WAVES and WAR

KEVIN MOORE

Waves and War: A Short Story

Copyright © 2012, 2025 by Kevin Moore.

First published in 2012 under the title "Waves and War." Revised edition published in 2025 as "Waves and War: A Short Story."

This is a work of fiction. Names, characters, places, and incidents are either products of the author's imagination or are used fictitiously. Any resemblance to actual events, locales, or persons, living or dead, is entirely coincidental.

For permission requests, contact the author through: unnaturalohio@gmail.com

Paperback ISBN: 9798999912602

Ebook ISBN: 9798999912619

Cover Image: *The Battle of Lake Erie*. Painting by Julian O. Davidson, 1887.

DON'T GIVE UP THE SHIP Flag, Alex Microbe, 2018.

Printed in the United States of America

Researcher's Note

The inspiration for "Waves and War" was derived from research conducted on the role of Northwest Ohio in the War of 1812, most notably: *The Naval War of 1812* by Theodore Roosevelt, *1812: The War that Forged a Nation* by Walter Borneman, and a visit to the Erie Maritime Museum in Erie, Pennsylvania which houses a full-sized replica of the *USS Niagara*. The outstanding first-person portrayal of Commodore Perry by Jeremy Meier, Chair of Fine and Performing Arts at Owens Community College, was also influential in the writing of this story.

Acknowledgements

Thank you first and foremost to my wife, Bethany Moore, for the original cover design of "Waves and War." Special thanks also to my colleague and friend, Carl Dietrich, as well as Mike Hornyak, author of *These Old Familiar Rooms* and *The Dictionary Game*, for taking the time to edit the original manuscript for this short story.

Also by Kevin Moore

Fiction
The Golden Merra

Nonfiction
Unnatural Ohio: A History of Buckeye Cryptids, Legends, and Other Mysteries (coauthored with M. Kristina Smith)

Short Stories
Seven Out: A Wil Driscoll Adventure
Waves and War
Sorrow and Demons
My Lovely Wife, Edith

September 10, 1813

My Dearest Abigail,

The hour draws nigh. As the gray dawn broke over the horizon, those of us on the first shift were alerted to the cry of "Sails ho!" from the mast. And behold! far to the North, the topman's spyglass showed the British fleet sailing from Amherstburg in Upper Canada. Thank the Almighty above, we saw only six vessels — two tall ships, one brig, two schooners, and a sloop — an inferior fleet to our nine boats, though, we are all of us concerned that our two-mast flagship is but a small brig hastily and pitifully armed. Pray the Lord is with us, for we raised anchor and filled our sails regardless. Light winds took us southeast of Kelley's Island before we turned north to intercept the fleet. It has been a long six hours since we spotted the enemy, and the Commodore has given us leave for rest and one last meal. But I am too unnerved to eat and choose to write.

Abigail, I beg your forgiveness. When war was declared, I was all too eager to join. I was a fool. I am a farmer, not a sailor. When the British seized Brother Patrick at sea last year, I was filled with such rage, much like the rest of our great country. The whole nation was like a pit of angry vipers! I ignored your protests because I thought the war would end quickly. How wrong I was! I thought the Army could storm the Canadian frontier and force a speedy surrender. Then I could return home knowing you and the baby would be safe. But the militias refuse to march into foreign lands, and the western front would have been all but lost had it not been for General Harrison's courageous stand at Fort Meigs on the Maumee.

The British have total control of Lake Erie, and now we are expected to take it from them. Any hope of supplying the Northwest with men and arms depends on it. But how can we do this, my love? The Lake Ontario effort has been well-armed and well-funded from the very first but has only met defeat. How is a pathetic hodgepodge fleet such as we expected to carry the day?

You can be sure the Commodore would have me thrown in stocks if he knew I was letting you in on the particulars of our dire complexion. But if your eyes ever see this, then I suppose that means I have gone to the hereafter where no punishment of man could ever reach me. I say these things because I want you to know that you were right, that here I am on this cursed lake proved a fool. And if ever there was a way to choose a different path————

With undying love, your Husband,

Joshua

The furiously ringing bell on the deck of the brig *USS Lawrence* sent shivers running down Joshua's spine. The time had come. After hastily signing his letter to his wife, he rolled it tight, slipped it into a glass bottle, and tapped the cork down hard. Joshua kissed the cool glass and held it up for a sacred moment. Should he die and the *Lawrence* be destroyed, he prayed Divine Providence would carry the bottle on its way to the lake's surface, to the Ohio shore, and on to his darling Abigail in Washington County.

Joshua hopped down four feet from his hammock to the lower deck and followed the rest of the crewmen who had been permitted to rest before the battle. He paused at the base of the stairs which led topside. There in a crate rested a pile of three dozen bottles, all containing farewell messages. It was the best position in the entire ship for them to escape through the main hatch should the ship sink. Two tears, and two tears only, wetted the rim of the dusty crate as Joshua placed his final words beside those of his shipmates. He wiped his cheek with a firm hand and marched upstairs.

A light breeze and mild temperatures met Joshua's face as he stepped topside. He raised his arm to shield his eyes as they adjusted to the midday sun. The main deck was a flurry of activity, even with a third of the 150-man crew still below deck and sick with dysentery. Joshua's boots crunched over freshly laid sand as he moved aside for the next man to climb out of the hatch. He cringed at the thought of the sand; the crew laid it down for traction when blood made the deck slick and dangerous. Men in tan shirts, like his own, scurried between the ship's carronades and climbed up and down the twin masts, while a select few in the dark blue uniforms of officers calmly surveyed the work being done, occasionally offering the motivational, "Look alive there!" or "On the double, men. On the double!"

The ship's bell still rang with urgency, and Joshua ran up to the starboard bow and leaned over the side. His eyes followed two and a half miles of deep blue lake water, a welcomed relief from the sediment-tainted green murk of the lake's western basin, to the closing British fleet. Sailing in a straight line, their smallest schooner led the charge followed by their stalwart and easily recognized three-mast flagship, the *HMS Detroit*, on her maiden voyage after the Americans had set fire to the last ship to bear her name. In the *Detroit's* wake, there sailed a stout-looking brig, a second three-mast tall ship and two runts bringing up the rear. All of the vessels boldly waved the Union Jack high atop their masts.

Joshua looked over the *Lawrence's* bow to examine

the American fleet. But where he expected to see the great *USS Niagara* in the lead, he saw only the twin schooners, *Ariel* and *Scorpion*. This was not the formation that had set sail from their anchorage at South Bass Island. Joshua climbed up on the starboard rail, clinging tightly to a taut backstay line, and gazed past the *Lawrence's* stern. The small brig *Caledonia* sailed in their wake followed by the two-mast *Niagara*. A medley of four schooners and sloops protected the rear flank. To Joshua's surprise, the *Lawrence* was the big ship out in front.

Joshua turned to the nearest crewman, a young man around twenty years-old whom Joshua was not acquainted with and who was in the process of lugging a thirty-two-pound cannonball to his gun. "Say, crewman!" said Joshua. "We're in the van?"

The deckhand set the ball on the deck and put his foot on it to keep it from rolling with the movements of the ship. He wiped the sweat from his brow and looked up. "Aye, we're in the lead. The British changed formation. The Commodore moved us up to engage the *Detroit*."

"I don't suppose Commodore Elliott will take too kindly to that, will he?"

Commodore Jesse Duncan Elliott had been in charge of all operations on Lake Erie until Commodore Chauncey, who oversaw the entire naval effort on the Great Lakes, appointed a replacement to seize control of the lake from the British. Being demoted to second-in-command was an affront to the man's honor, but at least he had been given command of the *Niagara*, a prestigious post to be sure, and a place at the head of the fleet. If they were victorious, posterity would remember the heavy ship that sailed in the van and little else. But now that the formation had changed, what did Elliott have to hang his legacy on? There was no glory for being fifth in line.

The crewman thought for a moment, grinned and issued a hearty laugh. But his laughter was stunted as two blasts echoed across the water. The crewman and Joshua turned to see smoke billowing from the bow of the *Detroit* as shots from her two long guns splashed harmlessly in the water several hundred yards short of the foremost American schooner. Still, miss or hit, the battle was on.

"Mr. Nelson?"

Joshua turned to see Lieutenant James Yarnall standing perfectly erect in his pristine blue jacket with his arms clasped behind his back. "If you would be so kind as to report to your station. We are at war."

"Aye, sir," said Joshua, hopping down to the deck. He made no attempt to apologize or give an explanation for foolishly balancing on the side of the ship as it sailed into battle. There was only one correct response to the lieutenant's command, and he had given it.

Joshua scuttled past Yarnall to the sixth of nine thirty-two pounders on the *Lawrence's* starboard side where the rest of his carronade crew was already assembled. Four men were required to effectively operate each gun. Two pulled on ropes to aim the carronade left or right while another, usually the eldest and most experienced, made subtle adjustments with the sight and the fourth triggered the gun's flintlock firing mechanism with a long pole.

"About time. How long does it take to run up some stairs?" asked Mr. Howe, the master sightman for the sixth gunnery crew. Past fifty years old, Mr. Howe's once black muttons had turned an ashen gray and his habit of indulging in mead showed prominently in his midsection. Mr. Howe was not a commissioned officer and he held no rank. To his higher-ups, he may have been no different than any sailor, but to his gun crew there was no question as to who was in command.

"Yes, sir," said Joshua, taking his position on the right-hand rope.

"Can't blame you for not rushing to get on deck," grinned the man across the cannon from Joshua. His name was Francis Harrison, supposedly a distant relation of the famed general currently holding his actions in the Great Black Swamp until news of the impending battle reached his ears. Joshua knew Francis fairly well since both men had been assigned to the Lake Erie campaign at the same time. They quickly learned that while they were both nineteen years of age, they had little in common as Francis was a rabble-rouser from Virginia enlisted by his father in an attempt to teach him character.

Joshua returned the grin as two more blasts echoed from the deck of the *Detroit*. All eyes aboard the *Lawrence* turned to stare helplessly as two black cannonballs flew across the water. The first ball ripped through the main sail of the *Ariel* with the shrill screech of rent cloth before crashing into the water just shy of the *Lawrence's* prow, but the second, whistling its malicious intentions a few seconds longer, pulverized the *Lawrence's* port railing, taking a chunk of timber with it into the lake. The whole ship shuddered with the impact.

The muffled barks of a dog, the Commodore's prized beagle, could be heard from below deck as he dutifully warned his shipmates of danger.

Fortunately, the glancing blow caused no injuries and most of the crew took the hit in stride, but some of the less seasoned men looked stricken. Joshua, Francis, and Mr. Howe had experienced cannon fire when the British had launched a failed attack on their shipyard at Presque Isle in Pennsylvania. But the gun crew's new triggerman, William Morris, began to shake uncontrollably as his complexion sank to a sickly pallor. Unlike his ambivalent relationship with Francis, Joshua had developed a strong kinship with William in the short time they had known each other and he now felt deep pity for the new recruit as he dropped the pole used to fire the carronade and wrapped his arms around his trembling body.

"Harden up, man!" yelled Mr. Howe. But the old sea

dog's reproach did little to calm the man's fit. The virgin crewman's contorted and fearful face reflected a total loss of self-control. Such was the case until a white gloved hand at the end of a dark blue sleeve firmly and reassuringly gripped William's shoulder.

"The Lion has barely begun to growl," said Master Commandant Commodore Oliver Hazard Perry. A man not yet the age of thirty, his voice was slightly soprano in pitch, youthful yet masculine, and reflected a hint of his Rhode Island roots. He lacked the rigid posture of Lieutenant Yarnall and wore his officer's coat unbuttoned at the neck, revealing the frills of his off-white dress shirt. A decorated bicorne hat covered his full black hair, and a loaded flintlock pistol dangled from his belt at all times, ready in a second's emergency. Descendant of a long line of sailors, he looked as comfortable on the *Lawrence's* deck as he would at home having a cup of tea, and his men admired him greatly for it. If ever he found himself alone at sea with no crew, those who knew him best had no qualms believing he could command a ship to port by only the sheer force of his will. "What's your name, crewman?" he asked.

"Morris, sir."

"Well, Mr. Morris," the Commodore said, putting his arm around the man. "Look at our mast. What do you see?"

"The Stars and Stripes, sir."

"And below that? Read it to me."

The *Lawrence* flew the flag of the United States high

for all to see, but below that fluttered a resolute marine blue flag that was unique to the Commodore's ship. Bold white letters emblazoned the flag's dark field: DON'T GIVE UP THE SHIP!

"Aye. 'Don't Give Up the Ship!' Do you know the story behind those words, Mr. Morris?"

William nodded. They all knew the story. The dying words of Captain James Lawrence as the British boarded his ship, the *USS Chesapeake*, had been echoed across every corner of the Republic over the summer. Every man aboard the ship that now bore the late captain's name knew how dear a friend he had been to the Commodore and how deeply he had mourned the news of his passing during their hardship in Pennsylvania.

"Then you know that unless the Almighty himself decree otherwise, this fleet will see the morrow."

The Commodore released William's shoulder, and the crewmen within earshot, now speechless, watched him walk away toward the bow. Two more shots rang out from the British long guns, but the Commodore's relaxed step remained unfazed. The cannon shot pelted the *Lawrence's* forward hull, but she held strong. "Accelerate the fleet!" he ordered. "Bring us in close for broadside. We're helpless under this long shot."

Midshipmen scurried up the mast to squeeze every ounce of speed out of the sails, the helmsmen held the ship's course steady, the communications officer ran flags up the mast to relay the Commodore's orders to the rest of the fleet and William picked up his dropped pole and held it at the ready.

With sails full of what little wind blew across the lake, the American fleet closed the distance between them and the British. The enemy's long guns squeezed in what shots they could before the Americans' advance made the forward guns ineffective. At half a mile, the British turned their ships in a tight arc to bring them parallel with the American line.

"Steady men!" shouted the Commodore as the British boats glided into view of the starboard carronades at a distance of about 300 yards. His plan was straightforward, and it appeared the commander of the British fleet had settled upon the same strategy. The *Lawrence* would engage the *Detroit*, and the *Niagara* would engage the secondary British tall ship, the *HMS Queen Charlotte*. The schooners in front of both fleets checked an attempt by either force to cross the other's line, and the schooners and sloops bringing up the rears impeded a flank attack by either party.

"Train left," said Mr. Howe, and Harrison pulled the *Lawrence's* sixth gun to the left. Mr. Howe sighted down the nose of the carronade for a moment before saying, "Train right." Joshua pulled on his rope, bringing the barrel about halfway back to its original position before Mr. Howe raised a rigid hand. "Perfect."

The stage was set. All was silent. Even the meager wind seemed suspended in anticipation. The two fleets and their commanders eyed one another cautiously, and only the gentle lapping of the water against the ships' bulkheads seemed unconcerned by the standoff.

Joshua secured the strips of cotton he had stuffed into his ears to drown out the imminent blast, and he barely heard the Commodore's words. "Well met. If you won't take the initiative, I will. Starboard guns, fire broadside!"

William tripped the carronade's firing mechanism. There was a flash and a thunderous boom, and the heavy iron gun lurched backward in a plume of smoke. One by one, the *Lawrence's* starboard carronades had fired from stern to bow, and all but two of their shots smashed into the *Detroit's* port side.

Seconds after the Commodore had given his command to fire, smoke also filled the *Detroit's* deck. The *Lawrence* shuddered as 140 pounds of iron slammed into her side. One ball, weighing twenty-four pounds and measuring five inches across, crashed directly into the ship's fifth gun, only fifteen feet from Joshua and his crewmates. The clang of metal meeting metal resounded fiercely, and the carronade was lifted off its mounting. Wood splintered in all directions as the long iron tube pivoted backward, flipped over its end and crashed onto the deck. The fifth sight master was too slow in getting out of the way, and the falling carronade crushed him instantly.

Joshua witnessed the whole ordeal. He had known the man. His name was Mullins. But Joshua had no time to consider his passing. He and Francis needed to shove another ball into the carronade in anticipation of the *Lawrence's* next volley.

"Prepare batteries!" ordered the Commodore. His command was redundantly echoed by Lieutenant Yarnall on the bow. The sixth gunnery crew, like every other crew on the line, already had their gun aligned by the time the order was given.

"Fire!"

For nearly an hour and a half, the two fleets exchanged cannon shot by the ton. Every vessel had taken its share of damage, but none as badly as the *Lawrence* and the *Detroit*. To look at them, the two flagships appeared equally matched in terms of what armaments still functioned and how many scars marred their hulls. But that equilibrium changed when the *Queen Charlotte* broke from its position opposite the *Niagara*, cruised past the stout brig in the center of the British line and heaved to behind the *Detroit*.

With her sails ravaged by grapeshot, five of her nine starboard guns inoperable and nearly half of her crew dead or incapacitated, Commodore Perry's prized flagship stared into the eyes of not one but two hungry predators. "Maintain all fire on the *Detroit*," ordered the Commodore. "The *Niagara* will engage the *Queen Charlotte*."

"Aye!" yelled Joshua in unison with his gun crew and

the rest of the *Lawrence's* deckhands. He and Francis set the carronade at Mr. Howe's direction until William approached to launch their next round into the *Detroit's* hull. Several blasts erupted from the *Queen Charlotte* and pelted the *Lawrence's* stern the instant William stepped up to the mark. One ball caught him square in the chest and carried him backward onto the deck.

"William!" cried Joshua. He had known William Morris for little more than a month, but they each had recognized the other as a kindred spirit at once. Joshua raised cattle on his farm in Washington County; William was a tanner in Marietta. Both had recently married and had had their first children: Joshua a baby girl and William a boy. Both were Quakers. Joshua played the banjo, William the fiddle. Memories of the last few weeks flooded Joshua's mind as he watched William die, recollections of the two of them discussing their plans to start a joint venture in Marietta when the war ended, introduce their wives and raise their children side by side flooded his mind.

"Don't lose your wits, Mr. Nelson," chided Mr. Howe. Blood streamed down his neck from his ear canals despite the precautionary cotton strips he had shoved inside.

Joshua's lips quivered and his eyes, which already burned from the blanket of smoke covering the lake, swelled red. "Aye," he bubbled in a tiny voice which was impossible to hear over the ringing that pervaded every crewman's ears. While tweaking the carronade's elevation to compensate for the ship's rocking, Mr. Howe snatched up the fallen pole and shoved it into Joshua's hands. "Now, Mr. Nelson," he implored impatiently after verifying his sight was still on target.

With icy and shaky limbs, Joshua extended the pole and fired the carronade. Tracking the ball through the fog was a fool's errand, but when the top of the *Detroit's* third mast, visible above the cloud of cannon fire, pitched forward abruptly and collapsed into the mist like a mighty oak felled on the frontier Joshua knew in his heart that it had been his ball that dealt the wounding blow. "That was for you, William."

"Reload!" shouted Mr. Howe.

"Yes, sir."

The crew of the sixth gun went back to work as urgent footfalls raced across the deck from the stern. "Commodore! Commodore!" As a panting crewman slowed his sprint to a trot, the Commodore turned with his hands clasped tightly behind his back. The restrictive collar of his shirt was now undone, and his hat was gone. One might have wrongly assumed the Commodore's loosened garb meant he was at ease, but one glance at the intensity etched upon his face showed that every one of his senses was plugged directly into the operations of his ship. "Commodore, the *Niagara* is holding. She did not follow the *Queen Charlotte.*"

"Signal them."

"We are, sir, but there is no way they can see our flags through this smoke."

The Commodore returned his gaze toward the twin British tall ships staring down upon his wreck of a brig. "Damn this, Elliott, where are you?"

For nearly another hour, the *Detroit* and the *Queen Charlotte* had their way with the *Lawrence*. The seafaring reapers claimed eight in ten of the flagship's crew. The immobile *Lawrence* began to list slightly to starboard, making it all the more difficult for its only operational carronade, that of Mr. Howe and his crew, to score a hit on the mutilated but still able-bodied *Detroit*.

"Load ball!" shouted Mr. Howe.

"Only two balls left," warned Francis.

"Then we'll scavenge the derelict guns for more shot," returned Mr. Howe.

"*Niagara* ho!"

Francis and Mr. Howe paused their exchange and traded smiles when they heard the topman's cry. That ecstatic and long-awaited call drew a cheer from every man yet able to hear. In an instant, the bloodied and haggard faces of the *Lawrence's* survivors no longer bore the dismal anticipation of death but instead a guarded hope.

"At last," yelled Francis as he pulled the gun barrel in his direction.

"But I fear it may be too little too late," replied Joshua. For the last hour, he had performed his job aboard the

Lawrence with all the vigor and honor expected of him, but inside he had been counting down the minutes until even the iron-willed Commodore yielded and ordered the ship to strike her colors. He had heard the horror stories of men detained in British prisons and of those violently impressed into His Majesty's service on the High Seas, but he had never dreamed he would see himself become one of those stories.

As if sensing Joshua's despair from half the ship's length away, the Commodore marched directly to the sixth gun. "You three have earned your stations this day. Abandon the guns and ready a longboat." Then, turning to the first crewman he saw, the Commodore shouted, "And you, Mr. Faulk, I need a fourth. Join them."

Another chorus of booms resounded from the *Detroit*, and a hail of two-inch grapeshot riddled the *Lawrence's* main sail, killing one of the topmen. With a wail, the man fell from his perch on the yardarm into the water. "Are we evacuating, Commodore?" asked Mr. Howe with a disciplined calm, as if the preceding spectacle had not occurred.

"I've never shrunk away from a fight in my life, Mr. Howe. Readying for the second round is all," answered the Commodore. "Lieutenant Yarnall, my flag!"

The thrice-wounded lieutenant, clutching a limp and bloodied arm, called back from the *Lawrence's* port side, "Should I strike our colors?"

"Don't you dare, Lieutenant. Let those Stars and Stripes fly!"

Joshua, Francis, Mr. Howe and crewman Faulk scrambled to a longboat affixed to a hoist off the ship's starboard aft. Their journey was a tumultuously slippery one despite the sand. The Commodore joined them inside the cutter as Lieutenant Yarnall finished lowering the Commodore's "Don't Give Up the Ship!" flag. The lieutenant approached the boat and handed the Commodore the blue cloth in a rumpled ball, circumstances not permitting a proper triangular folding.

"She's in your hands, James," said the Commodore. "Remember, you are now responsible for the welfare of this crew. And that includes my dog."

Lieutenant Yarnall smiled. It was the first time Joshua had ever seen the humanity underneath the by-the-book officer's uniform. "I'll keep them safe," the lieutenant said. "Lower longboat!"

With the *Lawrence* swaying, the longboat collided with the ship's hull multiple times on its way down to the rollicking lake. Joshua and his comrades, seated two by two, held their oars vertically until the Commodore gave his directions.

"Let starboard oars fall."

"Let port oars fall."

"Stroke!"

With each shout of "stroke," the tiny boat inched

farther from the *Lawrence* through water stained a grotesque shade of pink. Another barrage ravaged the towering flagship, and splinters of wood rained down on the five men. "Steady men," urged the Commodore. "Stroke!"

The longboat cleared the stern of the *Lawrence* and turned slightly for the *Niagara*, which was still too far away to engage either the *Detroit* or the *Queen Charlotte*. More explosions roared from the British side, and suddenly the water around the longboat became a tumult of chaos like a puddle in a thunderstorm. "No doubt they've spotted us now," said Francis, rowing with all vigor.

A splash erupted off the longboat's port bow, and a rippling swell lifted the boat out of the water before gravity brought it crashing back down into a trough. The resulting spray bombarded the exhausted seamen. Soaked from head to toe, Joshua gulped for air after the force of the passing wall of seafoam had overwhelmed his face and chest. He had little time to analyze their situation, but what had happened was sickeningly clear. The *Queen Charlotte* had fired a full broadside at their seventeen-foot, five-man flagship, and the near miss of only one of those cannonballs had nearly killed them. He knew they would not survive the next volley. "There's still two hundred yards to the *Niagara*. We're not going to make it!" he cried.

With the boat pitching back and forth and side to side, cannon shot screaming overhead and the very air of death so tangibly close, the Commodore did the most unlikely of things. He stood. "Row, Mr. Nelson. Row, Mr. Howe. Curse your mothers, row!"

"He mocks them!" yelled Faulk in disbelief.

More twenty-four-pound balls splashed within feet of the five-man crew, and spray doused them in sheets. The swelling water settled in the bottom of the boat and made it ride ever lower in the water in its desperate trek for the *Niagara*. The boat leaned to port then to starboard, and each time it looked as if it might capsize.

But the Commodore stood steadfastly upright on the stern like a monument of iron. Waves and war surrounded them, but Joshua kept his eyes locked on the Commodore. The Commodore's strength gave him strength. He pulled on his oars with every ounce of might left in his dead arms. "Less than one hundred yards, gentlemen," said the Commodore as the boat rolled turbulently through the wake of another sunken cannonball.

"Lest I be mistaken, Commodore, you appear to be having a good time," observed Mr. Howe.

"You're closer than you think, Mr. Howe," replied the Commodore. Joshua thought he spied the hint of a grin at the corner of his mouth. "Forward!"

As if propelled on the wings of seraphs, the impromptu flagship made up the remaining distance in great haste and without injury. Three lines dropped over the side of the *Niagara*, and the crew clambered up the side of the fresh and nearly unscathed brig.

"Welcome aboard, Master Commandant," said Commodore Elliott. A man of average height, he stood a head shorter than the Commodore. He wore his marine blue uniform stiffly buttoned and his cap firmly atop his head. His pale green eyes darted back and forth below his ginger eyebrows, shifting their focus between the Commodore and his valiant crew. "Per your orders, sir, I maintained the line and kept the *Niagara's* place—"

"Thank you for keeping the ship pristine, Mr. Elliott," said the Commodore. He breezed past the fleet's second-in-command and addressed the *Niagara's* crew, "I am assuming command of this vessel. Set full sail and pass the *Lawrence* on her port side. Keep us away from those guns!"

A chorus of "Ayes" echoed across the deck as every crewman set to work. The Commodore continued, still facing the heart of his new flagship with his back towards Elliott, "Mr. Elliott, take the four lads on your sixth gun into the longboat. Row to the rear of the fleet and rally the gunboats to the fore. I will need their support."

There was a long silence before Elliott replied. Joshua watched, feeling too small to make the slightest movement in the presence of the officers' exchange. It seemed to him as if Elliott's face had either slackened in incredulity or was paralyzed with rage. The Commodore waited, neither turning nor acknowledging his junior officer's silence, until Elliott at last shuffled away to collect his crew.

"Begging your pardon, Commodore," said Mr. Howe, stepping forward and filling the space formerly occupied by Elliott, "but do you mean to sail into battle short a gun?"

The Commodore turned slightly and gestured with an open hand in the direction of the newly vacant carronade. "Gentlemen, do what you do best."

"Yes, sir," replied an enthusiastic Mr. Howe.

Joshua was eager to rejoin the fight and smiled as Mr. Howe began barking orders and the Commodore left to shout his own. The sixth gunnery crew fell into their traditional roles with the exception of Faulk assuming the position of their fallen shipmate.

The *Niagara's* full sails caught the light breeze and the new flagship crept past the derelict *Lawrence*. The *Queen Charlotte's* carronades tried desperately to clip the escaping *Niagara* but to no avail. Disheartened, the British gun batteries returned their attention to the defenseless *Lawrence* as the receding American ship slipped deep within the blanket of smoke. The Commodore hoisted his personal battle flag up the mast.

Upon seeing that command had successfully been transferred, Lieutenant Yarnall onboard the *Lawrence* raised the white flag of surrender. Disarmed and taking on water, the vessel was completely useless, and the lieutenant's decision earned a nod of approval from the observing Commodore.

The roar of cannon fire died, and a cheer broke through

the soupy haze from the deck of the *Detroit*. The *Niagara* picked up speed and cleared the *Lawrence's* bow as the sound of celebratory British pistols being shot skyward reached their ears. "They think the Commodore has retreated," said Francis with a smile.

"Let them think it," returned Mr. Howe.

The *Niagara* pushed to the very point of the fleet past the tattered *Ariel* and the now mast-less *Scorpion*, both oblivious to the *Lawrence's* surrender and entangled in their own private firefight with the British forward schooners. "Hard to starboard!" cried the Commodore as soon as the brig was clear.

The deck bobbed as the bow split the waves, and the ship lurched to one side. Joshua held onto the deck railing for support as the *Niagara's* two helmsmen executed the sharp turn. Ignoring the engaged schooners protecting the British van, the *Niagara* sailed in a wide arc to pierce the British line.

The jubilant cheering aboard the *Detroit* stopped abruptly as the charging *Niagara* materialized from the fog. The British tall ship hastily fired off two rounds with their forward long guns, but at such close range both balls soared high and wide.

"Ready starboard guns," ordered the Commodore.

"Train left," urged Mr. Howe, sighting their carronade on one prominent point. The Commodore held his command until the *Niagara's* midsection lined up precisely with the *Detroit's* bow, forming at sharp "T." The crew stood silent, breath caught in their chests. The Commodore's crew was at that moment so fixated on their commander that they merely needed to see the softly spoken word appear on his lips. "Fire."

A chorus of booms made the ship shudder as a fresh crew with fresh guns raked the bow of the *Detroit*. Splinters and chunks of timber erupted from the enemy vessel like pellets of hail carried in a storm.

As the *Niagara* continued its arc behind the enemy line to the *Detroit's* starboard side and Joshua worked with Francis to reload their gun, he knew the Crown's champion was still a contender to be reckoned with. With control of the primary supply line to the war's western theater at stake, the British would not take the Americans' shot to their nose lying down. Whoever commanded the *Detroit* was no novice about to let his ship get pinched between the Commodore and the American fleet. With splinters still fluttering to the lake like blood trickling from a split lip, the *Detroit's* crew raced to open her sails, and the ship began moving forward with a starboard bent. All eyes aboard the *Niagara* tracked their enemy's trajectory, but Mr. Howe was the first to call out, "She means to follow us, Commodore. She'll be able to push us wherever she wants."

The Commodore, standing in close proximity, did not appear to hear him. In fact, he did not appear concerned with the *Detroit's* pursuit maneuver whatsoever. Like an immoveable sentinel, he stood gazing across the lake at the wispy silhouette of the *Queen Charlotte*, which was sailing only a few yards behind the *Detroit's* stern.

Joshua noticed the Commodore's lack of interest in the *Detroit* and averted his attention to the *Queen Charlotte* as well. Its commander had apparently taken up the same course of action as the commander of the *Detroit*. Filling her sails and turning to starboard, the *Queen Charlotte* mimicked the path of the *Detroit* almost identically. That is, except for two important factors — speed and angle of turn. The *Queen Charlotte* cut through the water faster than the *Detroit*, and her helmsmen made his turn too sharp. The *Queen Charlotte's* prow crossed over the *Detroit's* stern and ensnared itself in the flagship's aft sail rigging. Both ships, their wooden hulls groaning in protest, came to a dead stop as if stuck on a sea of glue.

The Commodore sprang from his stone-like repose and strode down the deck. "Fire, fire, fire! Reload, reload! Give them everything we have."

Joshua and his crew fired their cannon and prepared for another shot at Mr. Howe's discretion as the *Niagara* glided in closer for the kill. Like cogs in some kind of grand machine, each member of the four-man crew performed his task with deadly efficiency, and each gun in the nine-gun battery effectively devastated the trapped ships.

The crews of the *Detroit* and the *Queen Charlotte* tried

to disentangle their ships, but the complicated effort would have taken hours under the best of conditions. They tried to mount a desperate defense by firing two broadsides, but the majority of their cannonballs splashed into the lake. An unending wave of American iron poured in from all sides as the fleet's smaller ships joined the *Niagara*, and in less than fifteen minutes of the *Queen Charlotte* running afoul of the *Detroit* the white flag ran up the mast of the secondary tall ship. The commander of the British fleet struck the *Detroit's* colors immediately thereafter, with the rest of the fleet following suit in minutes.

Mr. Howe, in the process of sighting his next shot, was the first of Joshua's team to see the concession. "By God, they're surrendering!" Joshua let the carronade's rope fall limply to the deck and spun around.

The last few shots from the *Niagara* fell away as the Commodore ordered the crew to hold their fire. A collective cry exploded from the deck, "Huzzah! Huzzah! Huzzah!" Joshua pumped his fist in the air in time with the rest of the crew, and his heart raced more than it had during the heat of battle.

With the day won, the Commodore prepared to receive the defeated British commander, and the crew set to clearing the deck of the dead and wounded. Joshua was thankful he did not have to perform this duty onboard the *Lawrence*. As he and Francis carried an unconscious man with a long gash across his hairline below deck, Joshua's thoughts remained with the *Lawrence*, in the bin of sealed bottles. Abigail would never have to read his final words to her. She would never have to hold that dreaded letter delivered in the hands of an uncaring stranger. Joshua resolved that when the fleet returned to port, he would find his bottle aboard the *Lawrence* and burn its contents. He would also find William Morris' letter and keep it in a safe place while he counted down the days until he could return home.

Joshua still had six months left to serve and serve it he would. But he would not reenlist. The Battle of Lake Erie, as the men were already calling it, had been his first major battle, and he would be content if it were his last. Joshua was ready to go home. He would return to his wife and his farm, and he would deliver his friend's last words and the tale of his bravery to his poor widow. He could only hope that with the British fleet on Lake Erie now captured, his remaining months of service would pass by without incident.

Having dropped off the wounded man, Joshua and Francis trudged back up the stairs to collect the next casualty, but in walking across the deck they were stopped by the Commodore. "You performed a great and honorable service today, gentlemen."

"Thank you, sir," said Joshua.

"Aye, sir," said Francis.

"However, I must ask of your services once more,"

said the Commodore gravely. He paused sufficiently long enough to give them worry before he broke into a smile. "It is nothing dangerous, but I am afraid it involves more rowing." The Commodore handed Joshua a folded sheet of paper, and with a polite nod he turned away and walked toward one of his lieutenants.

"What does it say?" asked Francis.

Joshua looked down at the note. Its exterior was addressed to "General William H. Harrison; encamped at Lower Sandusky in Ohio."

Joshua caught Francis' eye. "How are you related to General Harrison again?"

"That has been a matter of debate in the family."

"Looks like you'll get a chance to ask him yourself."

Joshua unfolded the letter and read:

We have met the enemy, and they are ours.

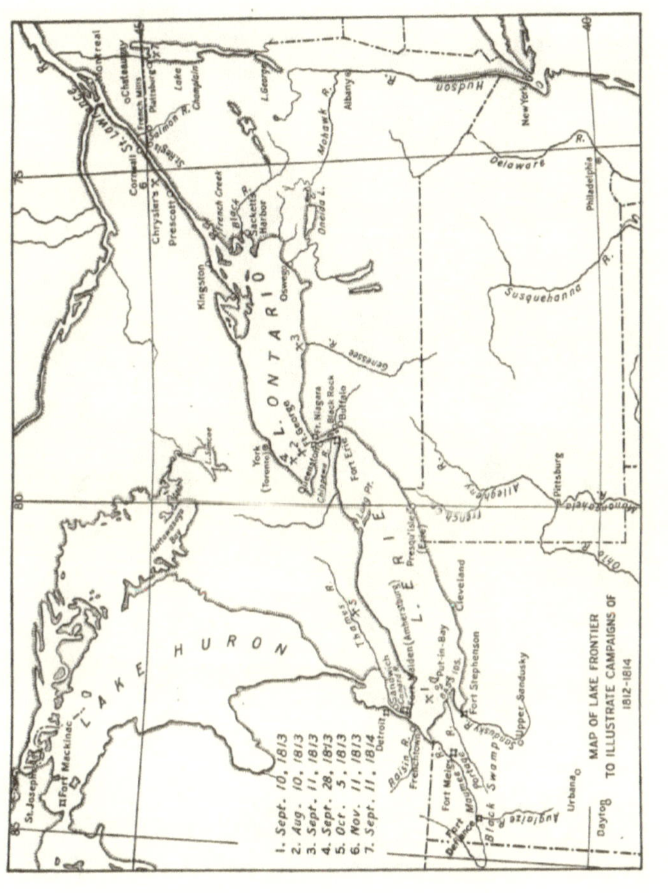

"Sea Power in Its Relation to the War of 1812"
by Alfred T. Mahan, 1905

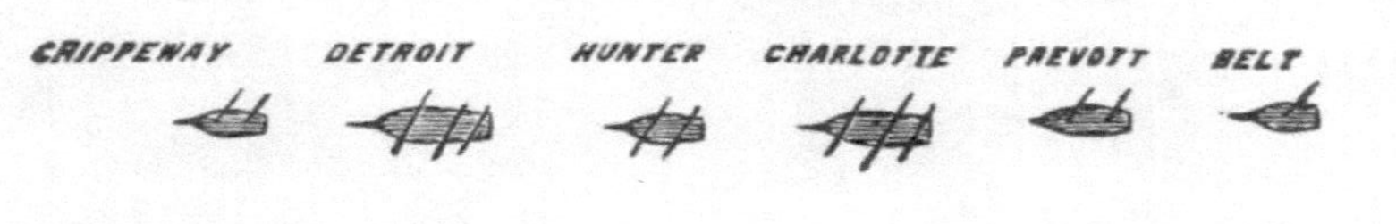

Ship positions at the beginning of the Battle of Lake Erie
The Naval War of 1812 by Theodore Roosevelt, 1897

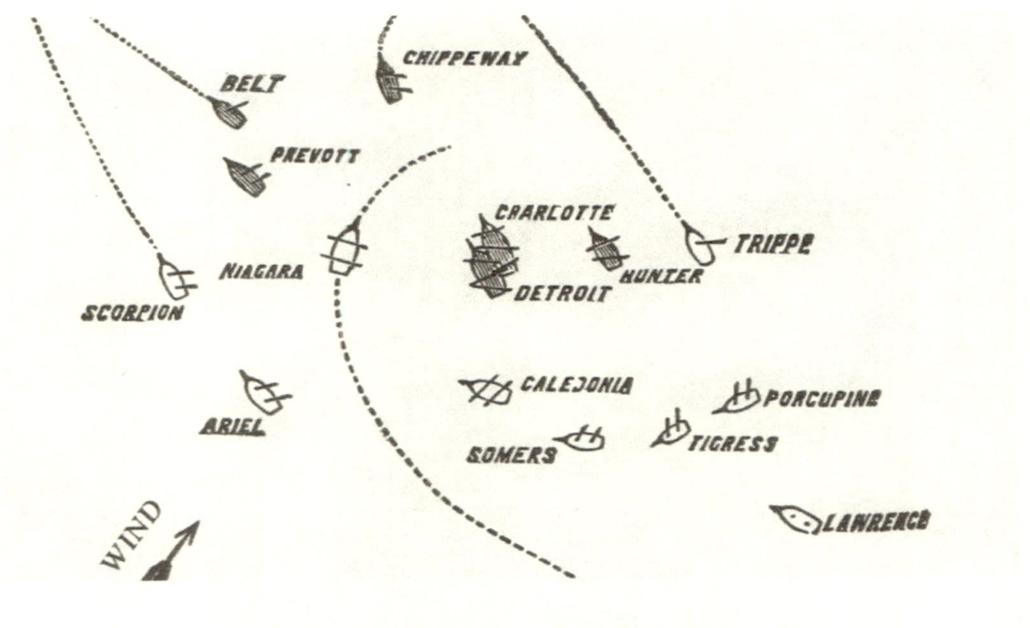

Ship positions during Commodore Perry's maneuver
The Naval War of 1812 by Theodore Roosevelt, 1897

Commodore Oliver Hazard Perry
Portrait by Gilbert Stuart, 1818-1828
The Toledo Museum of Art

Perry's Victory on Lake Erie
Painting by William Henry Powell, 1865
The Ohio Statehouse

About the Author

Kevin Moore enjoys reading and writing both history and fiction. He is the coauthor of *Unnatural Ohio: A History of Buckeye Cryptids, Legends & Other Mysteries*. He gets to research, preserve, and share history as the curator of artifacts at the Rutherford B. Hayes Presidential Library & Museums in Fremont, Ohio. He also hosts *Can't Make This Up: A History Podcast*, in which he has the privilege of interviewing historians and authors. Kevin lives in Toledo with his family.